RUFF

Guess what I want?

Written by Jillian Harker
Illustrated by Pamela Venus

Bright ☆ Sparks

"Guess what I want?" said Ruff to Rufus.

"Something from me?" asked Rufus.
"Now, let me see – what could it be?"

"You've got to guess,"
said Ruff.

"You want me to tie a string to the moon,

so you can pull it around like a giant balloon?" said Rufus.

"We could tie the moon
to the post of your bed,
to shine through the night
above your head."

"Would you really get me the moon?" asked Ruff.

"Well, it would be quite hard to climb up that high, but for you, of course, I'd give it a try," said Rufus.

"Guess again," laughed Ruff.

"You want me to catch you
a shining white star,
and capture its bright light
for you in a jar?"
said Rufus.

"It would twinkle all night and light up your dreams, and dance round your room, mixed with yellow moonbeams."

"Would you really fetch me
a star?" asked Ruff.

"Well, catching a star isn't easy to do,
but I'd give it a try,
because I love you," said Rufus.

"Guess again,"
laughed Ruff.

"You want me to capture the song of the breeze,
as it lulls its way gently through leaves on the trees?"
said Rufus.

"You'd be able to turn on the breeze's soft tune,
for the starlight to dance along with the moon."

"Would you really bring me
the song of the breeze?" asked Ruff.

"Well, the breeze moves so fast, it isn't easy to do,
but I'd find a way to do it for you," said Rufus.

Ruff thought hard.

"To tie down the moon, wouldn't be right.
And the sky is the place to leave the starlight.
It wouldn't be fair to stop the wind's song.
Now, try one more guess – your first three were wrong!"

"I know. I was teasing.
I think you want this…

...a huge great big cuddle, and a lovely big kiss!"

The
End